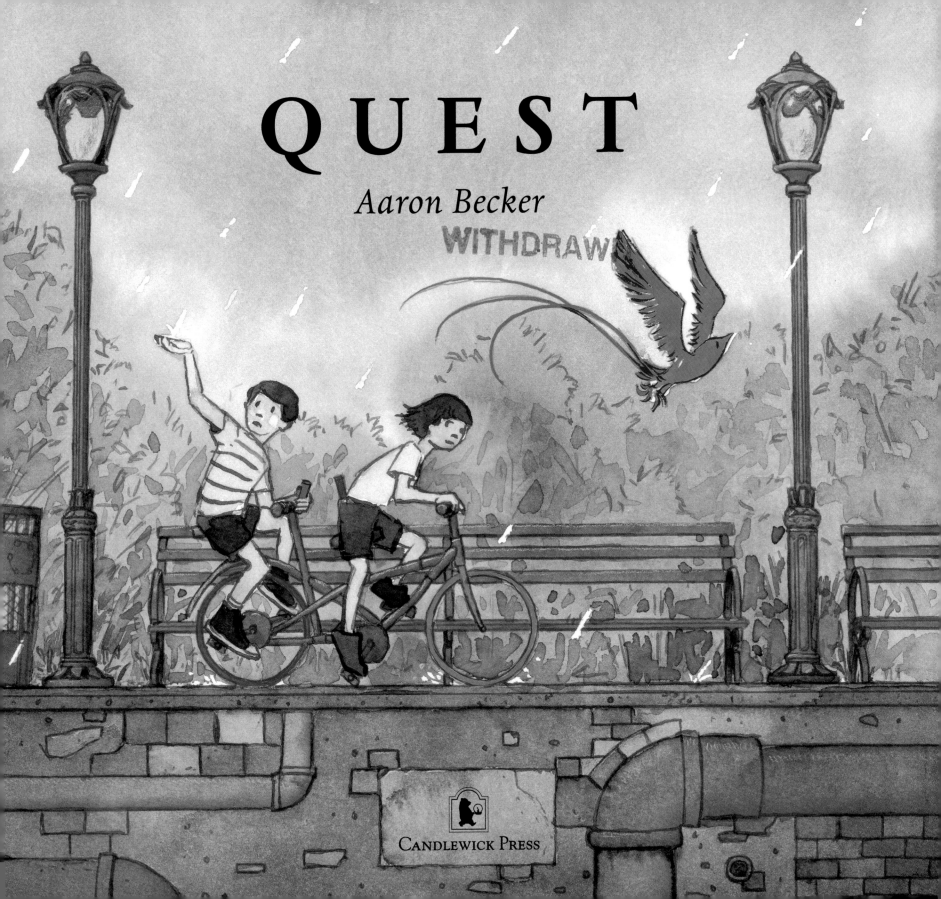

For Darci

First edition 2014

Library of Congress Catalog Card Number 2013952837
ISBN 978-0-7636-6595-1

TLF 19 18 17 16 15 14
10 9 8 7 6 5 4 3 2 1

Printed in Dongguan, Guangdong, China

The illustrations for this book were done in watercolor and pen and ink.

Candlewick Press
99 Dover Street
Somerville, Massachusetts 02144

visit us at www.candlewick.com

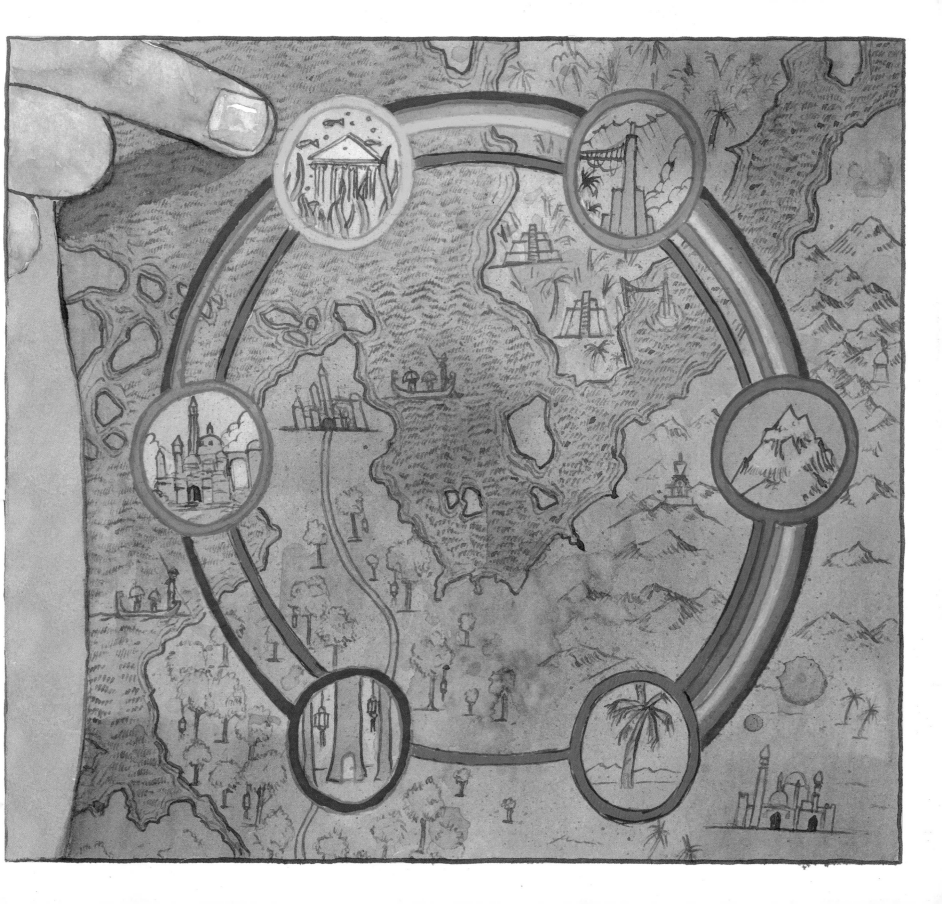